NO LONGER PROPERTY OF
SEATTLE PUBLIC LIBRARY

RECEIVED

APR 09 2023

BROADVIEW LIBRARY

# DANDELION TRAVELS

## ANGEL BARBER

An imprint of Enslow Publishing

WEST 44 BOOKS™

**Please visit our website, www.west44books.com.**
**For a free color catalog of all our high-quality books,**
**call toll free 1-800-398-2504.**

**Cataloging-in-Publication Data**
Names: Barber, Angel.
Title: Dandelion travels / Angel Barber.
Description: New York : West 44, 2023. | Series: West 44
YA verse
Identifiers: ISBN 9781978596139 (pbk.) | ISBN
9781978596122 (library bound) | ISBN 9781978596146
(ebook)
Subjects: LCSH: American poetry--21st century. | Poetry,
Modern--21st century. | English poetry.
Classification: LCC PS584.B373 2023 | DDC 811'.6--dc23

First Edition

Published in 2023 by
Enslow Publishing LLC
29 East 21st Street
New York, NY 10011

Copyright © 2023 Enslow Publishing LLC

Editor: Caitie McAneney
Designer: Tanya Dellaccio

Photo Credits: Cover (main image) huskdesign/
Shutterstock.com; cover (dandelion) Pavlo S/
Shutterstock.com.

All rights reserved. No part of this book may be
reproduced in any form without permission in writing
from the publisher, except by a reviewer.

Printed in the United States of America

CPSIA compliance information: Batch #CS23W44: For further information contact
Enslow Publishing LLC, New York, New York at 1-800-398-2504.

*For my parents, Mercedes and Daryl*

# MOM CALLS ME DANDELION

She says all the parts of me

　　　the darkest and lightest parts
　　　that make up who I am

travel around the world.

Carrying blessings and goodness.

Like seeds blown on the wind.

But she doesn't know me.
All that I contain and hold in.

Like the rest of the world,
she only knows
what I choose to show.

# LAST DAY OF JUNIOR YEAR

Thomas Gregory
is staring at me, Eric Wallace.
And it opens a hole in me.

> There's no Andrea.
> No Xavier.
> They aren't here
> to hold me down.

I feel my fist tighten.
I shiver at the thought
of what I might do to Thomas
all over again.

# ON THE FIRST DAY OF SCHOOL

Shiloh Fitz
walked down the hall,
carrying a sequined,
pink bookbag.

He was in the
wrong place at the
wrong time.

Thomas pushed him down.
Then spat the                    slur
that sends a                     chill
down every queer kid's           spine.

I felt protective.
Like a lion to her young.

My   limbs   moved   faster   than
my   mind.
My   fist   connected   to   his   jaw.

# THOMAS AND I

lock eyes now.

He makes himself smaller.
Then trips over his textbooks.

I close my locker door
and laugh inside.
Laugh at the power I hold
without ever raising my voice.

# I THINK OF MY POWER OFTEN

I see it in my classmates' eyes.

They look down at the floor
when I am near.

Terrified of the lies
spread by            Bloody Thomas.
Lies about           Me—

the        Angry        Black        Man.

The lies
that have haunted me
all of junior year.

I stay silent.
But still, they avoid me.

# I WALK

over to Andrea's car.
Her fresh nails
are pressed firmly
into the back
of Xavier's head.

Pulling him in closer
as they lock lips.

My stomach sinks.
But I still walk
up to the car.
Better to be with them
than to be alone.

I put on
my biggest smile
so they'll never guess
what I'm feeling.

# ANDREA AND I HAVE BEEN FRIENDS

Since before
my mom stopped
cutting the crusts
off my sandwiches.

United through
the soft comfort of
childhood.

United through
the sharp changes of
middle school.

Then Xavier spilled into my life.

# I THINK OF THE PAST

as Andrea drives down
    the twisty roads of our city.

I try to ignore
    her hand in Xavier's lap.

We wind up at our favorite diner,
    south of town.

    Mary's Diner.
    Our saving grace
    from the storms
    of the past year.

We always order pancakes
with extra syrup

    and feel better.

# ANDREA SIPS HOT TEA

slowly,
and asks about the beach house.

> *Have you asked your*
> *parents yet?*

Her uncle owns a house in Cali
overlooking the Pacific.
She wants me to come.

I tell her, *Not yet.*
*You know how they are.*

She rolls her eyes.

# ANDREA AND XAVIER

sit together in the booth.
He sets his head in her lap.
His sleepy eyelashes
brush against the fabric
of her jeans.

They sit as if they are

       the only two
       who exist
       in the world.

I excuse myself to the bathroom
before the tears flow.

# THIS HAPPENS SOMETIMES

My hands shake
over the bathroom faucet
as Xavier treads
through my mind.
I think of the first
time we met.
Two weeks before freshman year.
A party was thrown to
welcome the new school year.
We found ourselves upstairs.
I listened
while he drunkenly
strummed
his guitar.
The muddled notes
whispered secrets
about what made
him special.

He tired himself out
strumming,
and we kissed.

In the morning, he was gone.

# THE TWO LOVEBIRDS

met once school started.

Lovers,
almost three years
now.

I keep it together
so I don't lose
the two best things
that have ever happened to me.

I walk out of the bathroom.
Pretend I'm okay.

# ON THE CAR RIDE HOME

Xavier shows me
a photo of his favorite band—Thrush.
They've reunited.

*They're making a new album,*
he says excitedly.
*After 25 years!*

Andrea and I take a deep breath
at the same time.
Look at each other
and smirk.

We let Xavier's positivity
filter through the car.

He balances out
our tendency
toward the negative.

# I FEEL THE AIR CHANGE

as Andrea pulls
into my driveway.
It's like a black cord
wrapped around my throat.

Being around Andrea and Xavier—
watching their souls become
two of a kind—
breaks my heart.

But it will forever beat
the death grip I feel
as I walk from Andrea's car
to my front door.

# IT'S NOT THAT
# I HAVE BAD
# PARENTS

Mom and Dad
     (Tatiana and Stan)
have attended every award ceremony.

Been there for every high and low.

Showered me with every praise.

But I worry about how I look
when they are near.

I check my posture.

Relax my shoulders.

Make myself man enough
to be their son.

# MY FATHER'S BOOMING VOICE

I hear it as I walk
through the front door.
It turns my organs to seltzer.
*Where were you?* he demands.

*With Andrea and Xavier,* I say.
*Have you thought about the
beach house?*

He says we will talk tomorrow.

He holds my summer plans in his hands.

# THE MORNING COMES

My parents
are nowhere to be found.

Dad is a preacher—
he's busy making other people's
souls perfect.

Mom is an interior designer—
she's busy making other people's
houses perfect.

So my house is empty,
and I don't have to be perfect.

I feel the grip
of the black cord loosen
from my neck.

# AT DINNER

Father says,
*You're far too young
for a trip alone
to California.*

Father says,
*You cannot miss Greenway Row.*

And that is the end
of the conversation.

# GREENWAY ROW

is a church camp.
Five days a week.
Late June to mid-August.
A dozen or so kids.

Every summer since 13,
while my friends rode bikes
in the sun,
I sat in a dark, damp basement.

Made to pray to a god
I never fully believed in.

# I WON'T SAY

that I can't buy into God.
But he never sat
by my side to tell me
everything would be okay.

Instead,
my cries for normalcy
were met with cold air.

Every night before Greenway Row,
I'd try and talk to God.

But he never heard me.
That has never changed.

# FIRST DAY AT GREENWAY ROW

When I walk in,
the first thing
I smell is mildew.

I plug my nose
and try to follow the scriptures.

I think of Andrea and Xavier.
The jokes we would crack
if they sat beside me.
About the youth pastor's facial hair,
a goatee with a patch missing.

It makes time pass faster.

# THE NEXT DAY

I can't get out of bed.
I hear my mother
leave for work.
She probably thinks I left long ago.
Darkness licks
at my wrists and ankles.

I decide to stay home.

# NEAR MIDDAY

I hear my father,
who should be at work,
shuffling around.

The doorbell rings and
he opens it.

Heels clack on the floor.

A honey-sweet voice
fills the empty house.

I get up to see
the source of the voice.

I find my father
with a woman
wearing emerald earrings
and a long satin skirt.

My mother would say
it clashes with her
red sweater.

That sweater now
lies on the floor
of my father's office.

# I REMEMBER COMING OUT TO STAN

I waited for him to come home.
My nails dug into my arms
until they ached.

I sprung it on him
like a case of the plague.
The preacher's son
was gay—
it might as well
have been the plague.

He didn't yell at me
or say anything nasty,
but I could tell
he'd never look at me
the same.

I could tell I'd be expected
to hide it from the world.

As I walk away from the house now,
I think of what a waste
it was to worry that day.

He's the biggest hypocrite
of all.

# SITTING AT THE BACK OF THE BUS

I head for Andrea's place.
She's got her own apartment
even though she's in high school—
paid for by her rich uncle.
Her parents are way worse than mine.

The edges of my vision
blur with darkness.

Through a crack of light, I see my bus
pass Andrea's house.

If there's a God,
he must be playing
a cruel joke.

# ANDREA HANDS ME A PLATE

Grilled cheese.
And then a bowl
of tomato soup.

I tell her what happened.
Cheese sticks
to the roof of my mouth.

She comforts me.

This is a rare moment.
Just Andrea and me.
Without Xavier,
it feels like old times.

Like a wall has been removed,
and we can be
like we were years ago.

# STAN CALLS

The buzz of my phone.
feels like a shock.

He calls again.

I stare at the phone
for what feels like hours.

Decline.

He calls yet again.

I put my phone away.

# ANDREA DEMANDS

that I answer the phone.
*Let your father have it,*
she says.

*It's your place to scream,
cry, and curse. Show him
what he's done.*

But I could never do that.

Andrea quiets down.

# I WANT TO SCREAM

Break every family photo.
Laugh as the glass
shatters to the ground.

I remember being 11,
crying after skinning my knee.
My father looked disgusted
at my emotions.

Since then,
I vowed to never show pain
to him again.

Instead I just
shut down.

# THE PASTEL
# COLORS

of Andrea's apartment
remind me of my mother.

She'd lay out pastel dresses
on our ironing board
before date night with Stan.

Oh, the flames
that would burn those fabrics
if she had been there
this morning.

# MY PHONE DINGS

The text from my dad reads,
*Lucky's in an hour.*

I pick up all the pieces of myself.

Then text back
a thumbs-up.

# LUCKY'S

Just reading the name
fills me with memories.
Egg yolk pooling on plates.
Bacon sizzling on wet napkins.

My happy little family.
One that now exists only
as a memory.

# ANDREA ASKS

a question
that chills me
to my bones.

*What are you gonna tell your mom?*

Until this point,
my mother's pain
existed only in my brain.
It was manageable that way.

But hearing it out loud
turns the thought
from a feather
in the shadows
to a stone
in the spotlight.

I know I have to tell her.

# THE DOOR
# UNLOCKS

My nerves *zing*.
Xavier walks in.
Up to Andrea.

He grins, toothy.
*Hey, Eric.*
They hug and kiss.
Like a husband and wife.

I wonder if he would have
loved me instead
if his family weren't so
homophobic.
So many what-ifs.

My mind races
with thoughts of all
I may never experience.
And all the ways
I may be always alone.

*Can I have a ride?*
I ask.

# KNEES SHAKE UNDER THE TABLE

I'm at my family's favorite Lucky's booth.

How will my father feel sitting here?

I hope it kills him to remember
me as a laughing child
standing on the rough leather seats.

I hope he chokes on his own shame.

# I ORDER WATER WITH LEMON

I chew the ice slowly.
It calms my nerves
for a little while.

I see my father enter.
My teeth grind together.

My mother follows.
She looks sunken
and defeated.

I hold onto the edge of the booth
to keep from falling over.

# MY MOTHER GRIPS

my hands under the table.

*Dandelion*, she says
softly.

Then my father explains
his lies and affairs.

Stan says,
*Tatiana caught me
with another woman
a year ago.*

He doesn't say *sorry.*
He never says sorry
for anything.

My mother's face
looks like the face
of a prisoner.

It says everything.

# MY MOTHER'S HANDS

grow colder in mine.
My father keeps talking.

How he never meant to hurt us.
How he's acted ungodly.

The mention of God
makes me want to laugh out loud.
I get up to leave
as the anger takes hold.

I won't show him
my pain.

# MIDDLE OF NOWHERE

Lucky's is five miles
away from home.

There's nothing out here.
Except the breath of trees.
The rush of wind.

I close my eyes,
pretending
the dead of night
holds no trees,
no wind.

Nothing.

# CARS ZOOM PAST

Some coming home.
Others heading to the night shift.

I stand in between,
skipping through the middle white lines
as if I'm playing hopscotch.

Cars beep for me
to get out of the road.

The slightest gust of wind
could kill me.

And I don't care.

# MY FRONT DOOR

I debate going in.
I don't want to think about
what waits for me inside.

The door creaks as I open it.
Two pairs of rushing footsteps.
Two pairs of bloodshot eyes.

My parents stand in front of me,
united in their worry and anger.

I angrily push past them
and slam my bedroom door.

I hope they take the bait
and follow me in.

Fight fire with fire.

# I WAIT FOR THEM

But they don't come.
It's clear my parents
are giving me space.

This ticks me off
more than it should.

I've always been too much
and not enough
for them.

My body vibrates
with anger
under the sheets.

# A DREAM

I bask in the sun
on a beach
far from home.

The sun's rays
feel like kisses
over my body.

Then, I see a woman with
black curly hair
struggling to swim.

The waves crash
into her and I
jump up to help.

I fall straight into the sand.
It swallows me
whole.

The last thing I see
before going under
is the woman's face.

My own mother.

*Dandelion, help!*

# I WAKE UP STARTLED

I run to my mother's room.
I find my father
getting ready for work.

He mutters,
*We need to talk
at some point.*

*No, we don't,* I say.
I feel my power again.
All that pent-up anger.

I leave the room,
my father shouting
after me.

He'll never say the words
I need to hear,
so why bother listening?

# JUST KEEP WALKING

I get a text from Andrea.
*Meet at Silver's at 3?*

Silver's is a thrift store
in the heart of downtown.

The prices are low.
The finds are high.
My happy place.

I see a bus in the distance
and run to catch it.

# SILVER'S

smells of mothballs
and sweat stains.

The floor is always sticky.

The AC makes me shiver.

Yet every time I step
through the heavy double doors,
there's nowhere else
I'd rather be.

# XAVIER, ANDREA, AND I

never fight over clothes.

Xavier loves the 90s baggy
masc. look.
Oversized jerseys
overfill his closet.

Andrea is more feminine.
Baby-doll dresses,
pastels, edgy leather.

I like anything that feels
elegant and refined.
Burberry jackets and polos.
Classic, yet expressive.

# THE WOMEN'S SECTION

Andrea sifts through
the racks.

Xavier's eyes dart to a white dress
with lavender flowers.

I expect him to hand it to Andrea,
but he hands it to me.

*The flowers match your phone screen.*
A field of lavender.
A detail I did not expect
him to notice.

# THE LAVENDER DRESS

sits in the bottom of my bag.
I remember the first and last time
I ever bought anything feminine.

Two years ago,
we came to Silver's
after finals.

I saw a red leather
Fendi knockoff
that went perfectly
with a red polo top I got.

My father saw the bag
on the bed in my room.

I'll never forget
his look of disgust.

# I COME HOME EVENTUALLY

Where else would I go?

I shut my bedroom door,
praying for peace.

My father barges in,
my mother by his side.

He yells,
*I understand why you
are upset, but this is still
my house. You WILL respect me.*

His words are like daggers
detonating the bomb inside of me.

Boom.

The last thing I hear
before blacking out.

# WHEN THIS HAPPENS

When I am *this* angry,
it's like everything goes
black.

I'm suffocated
by my own anger.
I snap.
It's me—
but it's not me.

Everything I hold inside
all     the     time
just explodes.

So now there's
a hole
in the wall
of my once-perfect
home.

# THE LIGHTS ARE BRIGHTER

by the time I come to.

My father isn't here.

The look in my mother's eyes
reminds me of the panic they held
in my dream.

I cannot save her.

Or maybe I just don't
want to.


I grab my bag.
Pack what I need.
Leave for Andrea's.

# MY CHILDHOOD TOWN

is now too small
to contain me.

I spill out of its edges.

I run across town
to tell Andrea
I'm coming to LA.

# SIGNS

We sit in Andrea's room.

Andrea's in the middle
of Xavier and me,
booting up her laptop.

We go on the website—
one ticket left.
Headed to LA.

This is a sign.
I'm on the right path.

# THE RUMBLE

of this plane
reminds me of my father's voice
as he screamed at me.

As he accused me of disrespect.

It made me feel like the devil.
Like if I ever set foot in church again
I'd simply burst into flames.

But miles above him,
I can see clearly.

I will always be me.
He will always be him.

# IF I THINK
# TOO MUCH

about the floor of an airplane,
I get freaked out.
It's the only thing separating me
from falling 35,000 feet.
A plummet to my death.

Instead of thinking about Stan
or Xavier
or the floor of this airplane,
I think about the sun.

I think about how good
it will feel on my skin.

How lovely
it will seem after
the hell of home.

# PALM TREES

I've never seen one in person.

As the plane rides
down the landing strip,
the beautiful trees
are the first thing I see.

# WE'VE ARRIVED

Andrea's uncle, Frederick,
waits for us.

A tall man,
salt-and-pepper hair and beard.

He holds a sign:
*ANDREA AND FRIENDS*

He darts directly to Andrea.
They embrace in a calm bliss
only known by true family.

I wonder if I'll ever feel it again.

# FREDERICK WEARS VALENTINO

A crisp blue suit.
He drives a white Ferrari,
with custom leather interior.

Frederick is the only reason
Andrea has her own apartment
at only 18 years old.
Away from her toxic home
with her drunk parents.

But there's something lonely
about all his money.

In this six-seater car,
I think of how
the empty space
would crush me
if I were him.

I think I fear
loneliness
the most.

# FRUIT STANDS

As we drive,
the first new thing
I notice are the
fruit stands.

We don't have fruit stands
back home.

Pineapples

      Mangoes

Oranges

      Coconuts

I bet fresh coconuts
taste magical.

I promise myself
I will try one before I leave.

# THE BEACH HOUSE

looks out to the ocean.

I carry in my bags.
Frederick guides me
to my room.

Red walls.
Leather furniture.
Expensive design.

Different from the stale, pale walls
that haunt my home.

# ROOMMATES

My room is right next to
Andrea and Xavier's room.
I can hear them laughing
through the thin walls.

It's like nails grinding against a
chalkboard.

I push my pillow
over my ears
to drown out the noise.

# WITH THIS PILLOW

pressed against my eardrums,
I almost don't hear Xavier
knock on my door.

He asks,
*Do you want to go to a party
with us? Some of Andrea's
old friends from summer camp.*

The old me would've asked questions.

Who's gonna be there?
What kind of party?

But it's the perfect time
to dissolve,
to lose myself
in the chaos
of a city unknown.

So I go.

# I RIDE IN THE BACK SEAT

without wondering
where we're going.

Andrea stops the car
in the driveway of
a house bigger
than any in our hometown.

A glass wonderland.
I wonder how the owners feel.
Knowing people can see
every inch of their home.

I wonder if that keeps them
from keeping secrets.

# ANDREA
# ASSURES ME

*Xavier and I won't leave your side.*
He eagerly nods in agreement.

Moments before
my taste of adulthood,
I am stuck feeling like a child.

When we get in,
I decide to lose them
before they could ever see
I am gone.

# LOSING ANDREA AND XAVIER

was easier
than I thought.

Andrea was caught up
in the excitement of
seeing her long-lost friends.

Xavier was caught up
in the excitement of
being with Andrea.

I backed away slowly
as Andrea introduced Xavier
to the friends she'd made from
old summer camps.

# SHARP EDGES

I bump into the sharp edge
of a modernist table
and lose my breath.

A crowd of strangers.
Loud music.
An energy of joy.

But I am not able to enjoy it.

Andrea knew I would be overwhelmed.
I hate when she's right.

Everyone else sucks
the air out of the room.

I crawl to a bedroom upstairs
and try to breathe normally.

# I HEAR A KNOCK

at the door of a bedroom
I don't belong in.

I'm startled, terrified.

I'll be shunned from
the one safe space I've found
in the middle of this chaos.

The door opens.

A boy with a mess of blonde hair
and eyes the color of seafoam
is staring at me.

# ANGEL

My father forced me
to read the Bible
when I was seven.

This boy looks like how I always imagined
the archangel Gabriel.

He asks me,
*Are you okay?*
*I saw you run in here.*

A tender kind of concern.
Like he's known me for years.

I feel myself relax.
Say,
*I'm okay now.*

# HIS NAME
# IS ZACHARY

He knows Andrea.
He saw us walk in together.
He watched me depart.

He hands me a cup
of lukewarm vodka,
orange juice, and ice cubes.

He wears an old gray sweatshirt
from a university
I haven't heard of.

Loose-fitting jeans.

Our hands brush together
as he hands me the cup.

I feel a simple warmth
I've never felt before.

# OUT OF HERE

We go downstairs together.

We watch
Andrea and Xavier
dancing on the dance floor.

Zachary must see something on my face.
*Wanna get out of here?* he asks.

Yes, I do.

# I CAN FEEL
# THE HEAT

coming off of Zachary
as we walk on the beach.

So hot I think
the sand
will turn
into glass
where he steps.

The shards
will pierce my skin
as I follow.

# OCEAN

I look off into the ocean
and think about my mother.

Her ringlets bobbing up and down
as she drowns.

My chest rises and falls
faster than before.

Zachary puts his hand on my chest.
He slows everything down.

# ZACHARY STAYS LIKE THAT

His hand on my chest.

He asks me,
*What are you doing in LA?*

I pause to answer.

I could tell him
the whole story.

He might not get it.

I settle on:

*I needed the vacation.*

# MY PANIC ATTACK IS OVER

After I calm down,
Zachary seems to startle.
Like he's woken up from a dream.

I feel his hand
glide off my chest.

When the weight leaves,
I feel heavier.

He looks back at me
and for a split second,
he looks uneasy.
His eyes look darker.

*We should start heading back,*
he says.

I agree, but I don't know why.

My head sinks down
like a guilty dog.

# BACK AT
# THE PARTY

Andrea and Xavier
scowl at me.
Zachary and I
walk up to them
to apologize.

*You could have called,*
Andrea says.

> *My phone died,*
> I say.

*You could've told Zachary to call,*
she says.

> *I, uh, don't have your number,*
> Zachary offers.

*Why'd you leave in the first place?*
she asks me.

I shrug and keep the secret.

# THE RIDE BACK
# IS SILENT

Only hesitant directions
coming from
Xavier.

The GPS is only
making it worse.

Andrea sighs, annoyed.
She resents the idea that
she doesn't know
where she is going.

# THE JOYFUL SOUNDS

coming from
Andrea and Xavier's bedroom
don't make me as sick
as they did before.

I hold onto memories
of Zachary.

His hand on my chest.

I pretend it's still there,
lulling me to sleep.

# A KNOCK

wakes me up.
Xavier invites me to go
hiking with them.

Andrea, Frederick,
Xavier.

But I know
I'll only bring them down.

I politely decline
and fall back to sleep.

# ORANGE SKY

Sunset colors through my window
tell me the day is over.

Andrea opens the door.

*Have you been in bed all day?*

I tell her the time
must have
gotten away from me.

I don't tell her that sometimes
the darkness in me
makes it hard to move.

# I AGREE TO EAT DINNER

I see my puffy eyes
and disheveled hair
in the reflection of
the silverware.

I look over
to see Andrea
handing Frederick the bowl
of mashed potatoes.

There is a tenderness about it
reserved for blood family.

# BUT IT'S NOT ONLY BLOOD

Xavier also knows
this tenderness
from Andrea.

I can tell by the lightness
of the laughter
that comes from
their bedroom.

It makes me think
of Zachary,
his hand on my chest.

# A BUZZ FROM MY PHONE

I'm already in bed.
Normally I'd fall back asleep.

But something tells me
to pick up the phone.

*Hey Eric, it's Zachary. You busy?*

# ZACHARY HOPES

it's not weird.

Andrea gave him
my number.

I play it cool
and tell him it's fine.

Inside, I gush at the idea
that he could be thinking of me

as much as I am thinking of him.

# HE HAS
# TWO TICKETS

to the midnight premiere of
a new teen movie—
*Red and Rogue.*

His friend canceled.
He wants me to come.

Before I finish reading the text,
I am in my closet
deciding what to wear.

# DRESSED TO IMPRESS

I settle on
a crisp white tee
a tan blazer
blue jeans
and a silver chain.

My hands shake over the clasp
of my chain.

I think of
what to say,
and his car
pulls into the driveway.

I feel like I'm sneaking out.

Then I remember my parents
aren't here to tell me not to.

# ZACHARY'S RED CONVERTIBLE

smells vaguely of cinnamon.
Maybe it's his cologne.

He drives 10 miles over
the speed limit.

*we're gonna be late,*
he says, sounding stressed.

He hits the gas
a little harder.

As the speed increases,
I somehow feel safer.

# TWICE THE SIZE
# OF ANY THEATER
# BACK HOME

The smell of popcorn and
soda wafts around
the lobby.

We settle into our seats.
I nuzzle my head onto
Zachary's shoulder
to see what he will do.

He puts his arm around me.
The perfect date.

With the lights down,
we're intertwined
like two chains on a fence.

# IN THE MOVIE

A teen with rollers in her hair
dawdles in bed.

She waits by a blue telephone
for a knight to rescue her
from loneliness.

He arrives not in a chariot
but his father's run-down
Chevy Cruze.

These images of retro romance
have always felt foreign to me.

Halfway into the movie,
I become painfully aware
that the person holding me
is only a stranger.

He's not even looking at me.
I could be anyone.

Even here,
I feel alone.

# ZACHARY GLIDES DOWN THE HIGHWAY

like a knife through butter.

Everything about him seems easy now.

He puts his hand on my knee
and asks,
*What did you think of the movie?*

His touch is warm and strong.
But it feels alien to me.

He doesn't know me.
And why would he want to?

*It was fine*, I say.

We drive in silence.

# FAST

He swings into the driveway
too fast. Stops quick.

His hand never
leaves my knee.

I say,
*I had a good time.*
Unsure if I am lying or not.

He leans in to kiss me,
and I catch my reflection
in the car mirror.

All of a sudden,
I am my father.

I see his face looking back at me.
The hard lines on his forehead.
Cruel scowl.

I back away too quickly.
I look down at my father's
rough hands.

Zachary looks sheepish.
*I'm sorry if I moved too—*

My car door slams
before he can finish his sentence.

# I CALL THE ONE PERSON

who always calmed me
when I was younger.

*Hello? Dandelion?*

Mom's voice doesn't have the same
melody.
Instead, her voice is scared and pleading.
Like it walked across a tightrope
and lost its balance.

*I'm safe, Mom.*
*I just wanted you*
*to know that.*

*Please come home, Eric!*

*I can't yet.*

Not until I find
what I am looking for.

She starts to cry and
I hang up,

unsure of why
I called.

# SUPPORT

How does my mom survive
with no support system?

I feel an urge to call back.
To tell her everything will be okay.
To mend wounds I did not create.
To go back home to her.

But I cannot leave.

The black cord back home
may finally do me in.

# THE SALT AIR

that cycles through
the beach house
has turned stale.

I decide to go for a walk
the next morning.

I leave the door open
to welcome in new air.

A note on the fridge
tells the others where I am,
in case anyone cares.

# DIRECTIONS

To the north lies
jagged rocks of different
shapes and sizes.

At another time in my life,
I would have had fun
climbing them.

To the south lies
soft sand that opens
up to water.

I think of my mother,
the horror on her face
if I slipped and fell
onto a jagged rock.

I walk south
to the beach.

# I BURY MY TOES

in the warm sand.
It helps me keep my balance.

Looking out at the water,
I see myself in two different worlds:

The unknown waters
             and the sand.

The sand is solid and familiar,
everything I've ever known.

Maybe there's no love
for me there.

# I CAN'T DESCRIBE THE OCEAN

From my spot on the shore,
it's all that I can
never know.

I believe it has love for me.

So I jump in
with all my clothes on,

looking for something more.

# SINK OR SWIM

When I was seven,
my dad threw me into
a public pool.

I didn't know how to swim.

I gasped for air, but
his method worked.

I fended for myself.

Now I can
swim in the ocean
all alone.

# MY EYES STING

Salt water or tears?

I ignore
the burn as I push
forward.

The waves,
blue and menacing
push back.

My arms
grow tired.

In the distance I see
a figure swimming toward me.

# HER HAIR GLOWS

Crimson red.
Unnatural.
Magical.

She swims toward me at
an inhuman speed.

I slow down,
unafraid.

I feel like I'm where I should be.

Mesmerized.

When I look again, she has disappeared.
Yet the water feels a little warmer.

As if she brought me
a new life burning
with possibility
from the depths
of the ocean.

# MY MIND RACES

What could have swum
toward me at such speed?

*A fish?*

Maybe I mistook hair for fins.
I find it hard to believe.
A fish couldn't move with such grace.

Whatever it was,
I thank it for finding me.

I feel reborn
in these new waters.

A saltwater baptism.

# REBIRTH

I sit in the sun for an hour
to dry off my wet clothes.

I feel the salt
dry out my skin.

When I get home,
I lather on a layer of lotion
and lie in my bed doing nothing.

A rest to celebrate my rebirth.

I feel like God on the seventh day
of Creation.

# THE FIRST THING I DO

I pick up my phone
and call Zachary.

A retro romance move.

The sound of his voice
is like melted candy.

Sticking to my eardrums,
impossible to get off.

I ask him out.
*Show me the town
tomorrow.*

He hesitates for a moment.
Then says simply,
*Sure.*

# BEHIND MY DOOR

I hear Andrea and Xavier
joking around in the hallway.

I open my door excitedly.
Catch them off guard.

*What are you guys doing tonight?*

I ask. They look surprised.
I think they expected me
to spend the rest of vacation
in bed.

I did too. But that was Before.

*We planned a bowling night,*
Andrea says.

*Mind if I tag along?*
I ask.

That brings a smile
to their faces.

*Of course you can!*
they say in unison.

# RED DRIPS DOWN

Xavier's full lips.
The lips I used to
want to kiss.

Xavier gloats between bites
of a jelly donut.
*You guys know I used to be number one
on my middle school bowling team?*

Andrea teases,
*A lot can change in six years, love.*

She licks the jelly
off his lips.

He says,
*We'll see about that.*

# GREEN IS MY FAVORITE COLOR

So that's the color of the
bowling ball I choose.

The shiny surface reflects back
a sage-green world.

The ball is a few pounds too heavy.
But the green called my name.

I carry it to the lane,
and look back at my friends
who cheer me on.

Gutter ball.

But the loss doesn't bother me.

My green ball rolls
down the gutter with grace.

# XAVIER'S TURN

I study his form.

His feet are rooted
one after the other.

His fingers are
perfectly positioned.

He rolls a strike.

I look back at Andrea,
who sees through his victory.

She sees not a winner, but
the person she's grown to love.

I decide in that moment
to never chase love again.

To let it come to me.

# AT A NEARBY TACO TRUCK

We look out at the midnight-black ocean.
We sit on a bench and sprinkle cilantro
onto our floury pockets of meat.

*So,*
Xavier asks.
*What's up with you
and Zachary?*

Now Andrea is interested.
*Spill. Now.*

I have little to say.
I duck my head and say,
*Nothing...yet.*

I don't know if sparks
are going to fly.

I just know I enjoy
being near him.

# BACK AGAIN

*It's good to have you back,*
Andrea remarks
as we walk in the house.

I reply,
*A night out with you*
*patched me up a bit.*

*I'm so happy to hear that.*
*I've missed you.*

*This whole thing with my parents*
*really messed me up.*

Andrea shakes her head.
*You've been gone longer*
*than that, Eric.*

# HOW LONG HAVE I BEEN GONE?

How long have I not been paying
attention?

Did she see the despair on my face
every time she stroked Xavier's cheek?

The thought makes me sick
to my stomach.

I tried so hard to hide
the pain I felt
every time they were together.

I tried so hard to hide
the fact that I felt alone
even when they were near.

Perhaps my acting
isn't as good as I thought.

# ANDREA MAKES BREAKFAST

She sets heaping plates
on the table without a sound.

Xavier sits cross-legged.
Munches on bacon strips
and strums his guitar.

He lets his oversized Lakers
hoodie droop down to the floor.

Everything is calm
in a way it has not been
since I can remember.

I hear an engine outside
and rush to meet Zachary.

# PICNIC

Zachary opens a wicker basket
in the middle of a field.

Everything is my favorite color.

The green
        grass blends in with

the green
        of the grapes he has packed.

Best of all,

the green of his eyes
        when he smiles.

# WHAT DID
# I EXPECT?

When I asked Zachary
to show me around town,
I expected window shopping
on a trendy strip.

The last thing I expected to do
was lay around in the same kind of field
I could find back home.

But I see the content look on his face
as he tears apart blades of grass.
And there's nowhere else I'd rather be.

# NO SHAME

*I didn't think I'd see you again*, he says.
He doesn't look at me
when he says it.

I think back to our last moments
together.

I felt the hate of my father
fill up my veins.

Any shame I feel
is like a pebble in my shoe.

But I can just remove it
and walk toward what I want.

Any god watching me now
will have to turn away.

Because I grab Zachary's face
and kiss him like I
never wasn't certain.

# WHAT DID HE EXPECT?

After a moment,
Zachary pulls his face back,
his face red.

He says,
*I wasn't expecting that.*

I wasn't either.

# KISSING ZACHARY OPENS ME UP

I talk about my childhood.
The small details like
the red swing set by
the oak tree I swung on
as a kid.

He tells me of
the Italian wedding soup
his mother would make
any time he was sick.

He looks down as he tells me this.
Like it's hard to share something
so small and so personal.

# RELIVING MY CHILDHOOD

in this space of love,
or at least this space of *like*,
makes me see
how much I missed
whatever *this* is
in childhood.

When other kids were having
their first crushes and learning
how to let love in,
I spent my time
keeping everything
I felt
out.

# THEN SOMETHING HAPPENS

The ground seems to shake.
A weight hits my chest.
It feels like the sky is falling.

When I look up to the sky
to look God in the face,

I see Zachary instead.
His arms gently wrap around
me as I finally, finally
cry.

A lifetime worth of tears
kept inside.

For the first time
in a long time,
I don't feel alone
at all.

I feel in love.

# AT HOME

the days of summer
would blend together.

Shades of gray
mixing in a mournful sky.

Here, we fall into routines
that never dull the senses.

Andrea goes for walks.
Xavier practices guitar.

And I text back and forth
with Zachary for hours—
then sneak out to meet him.

My heart beats faster
and I lose my breath quicker
with each passing day.

# THEN ONE MORNING

I grab my phone,
excited to hear from Zachary.

But there's nothing.

I hold onto an image
from last night.

The two of us tangled up in
beach grass.

As the hours pass,
I worry images of Zachary
will fade away like the corners
of an old photograph.

# ACHE

There's something real
about this kind of ache,
something I can touch.

Something that never existed
with Xavier.

Every time I went to Xavier,
he was already with Andrea.

I knew it would never happen
between us.

But knowing that Zachary exists
and wants what I want
creates a home for him
within me.

I can see it.
I can feel it.
Even when he's not around.

# I WISH I COULD LIVE IN THE OCEAN

Side by side with my new lover.

We could find a spot
within a coral reef
and call it home.

The ocean covers 71 percent of the Earth.

There has to be a place
for us there.

# I SIT OUTSIDE
# ALL MORNING

Waiting for a text
from Zachary.

Andrea and Xavier are sleeping in
after a night out.

Frederick left for a business trip.

And Zachary is out of reach.

I try to remember if the little mole
above the bridge of his nose
lies on the left
or the right side.

# ALL THIS TIME
# TO THINK

makes me think about my dad.

I thought I was over it.
I thought I was over him.

But I keep thinking about how
he'd pick me up from school.

We'd listen to the live Jimi Hendrix album
in the car together.

It was the one time he'd seem content,
just driving around.

I'd sit motionless next to him
careful not to expose any parts
of me that might ruin the moment.

I knew if I just didn't say anything,
he could still love some part of me.

No matter how small.

# I GUESS STAN WASN'T ALWAYS BAD

Whenever I'd get good
marks in school, we'd
celebrate at Lucky's.

He'd order us a slice of
Bavarian chocolate cake.

His eyes would sparkle
as I scarfed down my half.

*My boy's gonna be something,*
I'd hear him say to others.

How can this supportive father
and a twisted beast
coexist
within the same body?

I go inside
so I don't have to wonder.

# ALONE TOGETHER

Andrea is on her usual late-morning
walk.
Frederick is still on his trip.

So Xavier and I sit
across from each other eating
Raisin Bran.

His eyes glow brown,
a sandy desert.
But they have
no power over me anymore.

He has the same fullness in his lips.
But I have
no desire to kiss them.

# I BREAK
# THE SILENCE

*How's the trip been for you?*
It's the first sentence I've spoken all day.

He perks up at the sound of my voice
as if he's been waiting for me to speak.

Maybe for years.

*Great!* he says.
He starts telling me
all about his adventures
with Andrea:
the beach,
long drives,
cool food trucks.

For the first time ever,
I see him clearly.

He is not my love.
He is a fool in love.

Young and hesitant,
waiting and hoping.

I envy the freedom
that radiates off of him.

# LIGHTER

*You seem lighter,*
he remarks as I
shovel a bite of Raisin Bran
into my mouth.
*I think Zachary has been good for you.*

I agree.
I even smile a bit.

I can now spend a moment of time
alone with Xavier without feeling
every cell pop in my body.

# ZACHARY FINALLY TEXTS

And I finally exhale.

Fear creeps down my spine.
Now I know how dangerous
he is to my emotions.

The slightest shift in him
could hurt me like
nothing I've ever known.

# BACK IN MY ELEMENT

Zachary takes me to a local thrift store.
This is where I'm meant to be.
Shirts, dresses, sweaters, blazers.
In every color and fabric.

My money has gone down to
little more than a small wad
of twenties.

I watch Zachary's hands flip through
sweaters with different textures.

Where have these hands been?
Where will they go?

How strange is it that I know so little
about the hands I seem to love.

There's a scar above his left pinky knuckle.
*How'd you get that scar?*

I am answered with silence.
He shuts down.

I leave the store with a mahogany blazer.
He leaves with a white-checkered flannel
shirt.

# ZACHARY IS
# A MYSTERY

Maybe that's what first
attracted me.

Sitting on the beach with
him that first night, there
was a darkness in him,
something both unknowable
and familiar.

At the time,
maybe I thought I had
the flame that could
light him up.

# AS IF NOTHING HAPPENED

I settle into the passenger seat.

*Where to next?* he asks.

He puts his arm around me,
as if nothing happened before.

Now he's my personal driver
with a rose between his teeth.

Showing me the lovely streets
of Los Angeles.

*Can you take me to your house?*
I ask innocently.

Zachary takes a pause.
My heart inflates.

*Not today,* he says.

Deflation.

# I CAN PUSH AND PRY

Ask him what's stopping him
from letting me in.

Or I can leave it alone.

I mean, I know we just met
a few weeks ago.
But he has to feel this too.

Ever since I've been here,
Zachary has only taken his mask off
a handful of times.

It was okay at first,
because I was closed off, too.

But now I'm open.
Ready to love.

The look on his face
as he focuses on the road—
almost a little sad—
makes me wait.

# MAYBE I'M
# A COWARD

I close the passenger door
a little harder than necessary
as I leave his car.

Why won't he let me in?

Why can't I form the words
to ask him?

Maybe I'm not good enough.
Maybe he has lovers sprinkled
across the West Coast.

Secret lives and layers.

Or maybe he's just scared.
Maybe inside, he's on his knees,
begging like a child
for someone to push
the door down.

# FREDERICK IS HOME

He sets his suitcase
on the landing of the stairs
late at night.

He leaves one bag out,
saying it's full of goodies.

A snow globe for Xavier.
A perfume for Andrea.

Last but not least—
he hands me a vintage wooden doll
with skinny arms and legs
and a big, round head.

*It made me think of you!* Frederick says.
*It's wearing the same sweater
you wore when you first got here*.

I touch the yellow cable-knit sweater.
The doll's sweater has black trim,
mine has white.

I thank Frederick and
take the doll into my room.

# WISH GRANTED

I was never allowed to
play with dolls as a child.

I would see them in stores.
Wish I could rip them
out of the plastic with my teeth.

But I could just imagine
the look of embarrassment on
my father's face.

The look of shame
on my mother's face.

It was enough to stop me
from asking.

Placing the doll on the mantel
of my new room feels like
a long-overdue hug
to my inner child.

# *WHAT IS LOVE?*

I stare at the doll
and ask it big questions.

In some way, it answers.
Or maybe I do.

Love changes and bends
at the will of each person.
Sometimes love is just
acceptance of another's love.
I will accept whatever love
Zachary decides to give me.

Whether it be a sliver of him
or the entirety,
I'll take it.

# SO I MAKE THE NEXT MOVE

I call Zachary.
Texting doesn't feel like enough.

I feel my fingers tremble
as I hold the phone.

*Hello?*
he says sleepily.

*Do you want to get dinner
tomorrow?*
I ask confidently.
*A real date.*

I know this could go
either way—
acceptance or rejection.

My heart swells when he
says, *Can't get enough of me?*

I can imagine his
toothy grin as he flirts.

A surge of fear hits again.
But I swallow it and say,
*I could never get enough of you.*

# AFTER I HANG UP

I see the dozens of
unread messages and missed calls
from my mother.

I listen to the first three seconds
of each voicemail.

*Where are you—*

*Eric, please answer—*

*Dandelion—*

I imagine a boulder crushing
my mother's chest,
the weight of a
missing child.

So I call her back.

# MY MOTHER'S ANGRY VOICE

*Eric?*

*Mom, I—*

*No. I need you to listen to me.
I don't care where you are.
You need to come home.*

*It's not that easy—*

*If you're not home in a week,
I'm calling the police.
You're not an adult yet.
Get home now.*

She hangs up the phone.

# WHAT DOES MY FATHER THINK?

He has not contacted me once.
Every missed call and text
is from my mother.

I wonder if the guilt is eating him alive,
knowing he caused all of this pain.

I hope it is.

# WIND CHIMES

Zachary's ringtone.

The melodic riff makes my
heart sparkle.

His text reads,
*Be ready in an hour.*

# CITRUS AND LAVENDER

I jump in the shower
and lather on citrus body wash.
Then moisturize,
Look in my closet to see
what I should wear.

I feel like that teen
in the movie.

Then I see the lavender dress.

I remember how Xavier
chose it just for me.

It calls to me, but I
hesitate to pick it up.

# I FEEL THE EYES

of every person
who has ever looked
at me in disgust.

They scan my body
all at once.

But then I think about Zachary
and all of the eyes fade away.
If I want to see the real him,
I need to show him the real me.

So I grab the dress and put it on.

Looking in the mirror,
I admire the way it hugs
my body.

# A SUDDEN SHARP PAIN

digs into my stomach.
Like I've been hit.

I look in the mirror again.
But everything has changed.

I feel like I'm in a funhouse
with mirrors distorting my body.

How could I have ever thought
this looked good?

The disgusted stares come back.

I feel them watching me
as I shift around in my clown suit.

But Zachary beeps the horn outside.
I have no time to change.
So I drag my feet to the car
with bricks tied to my ankles.

# THE WORST REACTION

Zachary looks me up and down
like a puzzle he can't solve.

*What are you wearing?* he asks.
The words come out
terribly slow.

He must see the slapped look
on my face.

*You look lovely, I mean,*
Zachary says. His words are fast
and I don't believe them.

*Thank you,*
I say.

We ride in silence
to the restaurant.

# A TEAR IN
# THE FABRIC

Our booth has a tear in it,
like someone took a knife and
slit down the pleather seat in a fit of rage.

I sit across from Zachary, who picks at his
fingernails and sips ginger ale.

He looks around the restaurant
and out the door.

# WE DON'T SPEAK

The table between us
has become a brick wall.

Our voices would grow hoarse
from screaming over the boundary.

We order food and eat it silently.

Then something behind me catches his
attention.
His eyes dart back and forth, nervously.

I turn around to see what it could be.

# A BOY

Zachary glares at him,
all his darkness coming up
to the surface.

Something primal and hungry.

Zachary licks his lips as if he's starved.

As if he hasn't just eaten
an entire bowl of pasta
and half of my cheese fries.

# MYSTERY BOY
# IS A WAITER

He notices Zachary,
then moves a hand through
his sandy blond hair
and sprints over
to our table.

*What are you doing here?*
he asks Zachary sharply.

*Enjoying some food,*
Zachary says with a shrug.

I settle into my booth,
confused by the mystery boy
leaning over our table in anger.

# FLASHBACK

*Can we help you?*
I ask as my irritation grows.

I can hear the anger
in my voice, the protectiveness.
Just like when I protected Shiloh Fitz
from Thomas Gregory.
*If not, I think you should go.*

The stranger looms over us.

Neither Zachary nor the waiter speak.
But the tension between them speaks
volumes.

I feel a pit growing in the middle of
my stomach, as I start to know things
that I never wanted to know.

When Zachary finally opens his mouth
to speak, he simply says,
*Robert, you heard the man.*

# ROBERT LOOKS DOWN AT ME

*Did you really think this—*
*would make me jealous?*

He spits out a racial slur.

My face gets hot.
Suddenly
        I'm aware of my skin.

How dark it is compared to the
rest of the people in this restaurant.

What they must think
of            Me—

the        Angry        Black        Man.

The last thing I think about
before blacking out in rage
is Thomas Gregory.

# BLOOD LEAKS

from Robert's face
to my knuckles.

Someone is pulling me away.

They are Zachary's hands,
but they no longer feel like a haven.

I look in the face of
every horrified person
sitting in their booth.

Their faces look shocked, but
underneath I know this is what they
expected.

Sometimes being Black is knowing that
no one cares when you fail—they expect
nothing more from you.

# ZACHARY IS QUIET

until we are halfway
to the beach house.

*I'm sorry,*
he says while reaching for my
knee.

I jerk his hand away.

# ZACHARY
# EXPLAINS

*Robert's my ex.*
*We were together two years.*

What he doesn't say
is how much more meaningful
their time together was
than anything we
could ever have.

Nausea hits
and I roll down
the car window

to let the salt air
soothe.

# I WAS A PAWN

A chess piece in Zachary's pathetic
attempt
to win back his true love.

Zachary explains,
*He had his moments.*
*He wasn't always bad.*
*I never knew he was capable*
*of saying such disgusting,*
*racist things.*

Zachary's words should mean
something.

Except I know that at the very first
chance,
he would
JUMP
back into Robert's arms,
forgiving him.

There's no way
I'm a winner
in this game.

# ZACHARY TALKS ABOUT ROBERT

with a lightness I did not know
he was capable of.

How he loses himself
whenever Robert smiles.

I bet Robert knows the truth
behind the scar above Zachary's
left pinky knuckle.

As he talks, Zachary's eyes beam
in a way I've never seen.

He has never looked at me
that way,
and he never will.

# PLEADING

I say nothing when Zachary pleads
with me to forgive him.

I look down at him like a dog.
I can see the tail between his legs.

As soon as he stops the car,
I jump out of it,
hoping to never see him again.

# XAVIER WAITS

alone by the door,
witnessing my worst moment.

He sees my tear-stained face
when I can't hold it in anymore.

*What happened?*

> *It was all just a game*
> *to win someone else back,*
> I say.

Xavier looks down the road
where Zachary's car has disappeared.

And I see the devil in his eyes.
He would fight for me.

It makes me feel cared for
in the most basic way.

Like when your mother
curses the sidewalk for skinning
your knee.

# XAVIER GRABS MY SHOULDERS

and tells me
everything
will
be
okay.

I look up at him.

I remember our night together,
years ago
when his hands
touched my shoulder
just like this.

# TIME ERASES

I feel myself
back in the room
where we first met.

He is three years younger,
with longer hair
and he still wears
thrifted band tees.

I kiss his lips.

But unlike three years ago,
his mouth does not move
against mine.

His eyes are wide and worried.

I pull back and turn around,
to see Andrea.

# THE WORST BETRAYAL

I instantly pull away from Xavier
in pure horror.

What have I done?

Andrea stands in the doorway,
looking betrayed.

I run away from them
in my lavender dress,
leaving chaos behind me.

# BACK AT THE BEACH

Angry waves beat against rocks and sand.

The look of pain on Andrea's face makes me sick to my stomach.

I rack my brain for reasons for why I did what I did.

I wanted to feel love.

What a pathetic reason to ruin the only true friendship I've ever had.

# THERE'S A
# MIRROR

in the bathroom at the beach.
My stubble has grown out of control.
The lines around my face have hardened.
They contrast with the beautiful
lavender dress.

I don't look beautiful.
I look like my father.

The reflection in the mirror
fills me with a primal rage,
and I pull out my phone
to call him.

# I UNLOAD

I blame my father
for everything that
has happened,
and everything
that will happen.

My lungs breathe fire
as I rant—

        and he takes whatever I throw.

I yell so loud I fear the mirror will break.

Eventually, my lungs grow tired,
and the line goes silent.

*Come home, Eric,*
he says simply.
*Please.*

It's not the words,
but how they sound
coming from his mouth.

I know it is time
to end my travels.

# TICKET HOME

Andrea buys my ticket
to go home tomorrow.

We don't say a word as she purchases
the ticket with Frederick's credit card.

Xavier isn't around.

I ask,
*So are we going to talk about—*

> Andrea glares at me.
> *Not now, Eric.*

After years of dealing
with my darkness,
even she
has had enough
of me.

# IN THE DEAD OF NIGHT

wind chimes wake me up.

I don't want to talk
to Zachary. Now or ever.

But I answer anyway.

> *Can we talk?*

I know I could ignore him.
But that's the coward's way out.

*I'm leaving tomorrow morning.*

> *Then let me drive you to the airport.*

*Fine.*

# DIFFERENT

Zachary's car smells different.

*I never meant to hurt you,*
he starts.

I feel nothing.

*I won't accept your apology
just so you don't have to
feel guilty.*

His face drops.

It almost makes me feel cruel.
I don't like the power I have
to cause pain.

But I don't deserve to be hurt, either.

# A BLOCK AWAY FROM THE AIRPORT

I see a fruit stand.

I remember my promise to myself:
to try fresh coconut before I leave.

I decide I will never break
a promise to myself again.

*Stop!*
I tell Zach.
His brakes squeal.

I don't say goodbye to him—
I don't need to.

# INSTEAD

I leave his car
for the last time,
and sprint to the fruit stand.

The man at the stand hands
me an open coconut with a pink
swirly straw.

It tastes so fresh.
Way better than the bottled water
at home.

I'm so glad I let myself
have it.

# GOODBYE TO THE PALM TREES

I look through the fingerprint-stained
mirrors of the airplane.

I sit in the emergency exit row.
I wonder how long it would
take my lungs to explode if
I opened the emergency hatch.

But I don't want to
die—

I just want to live
on my own terms.

# I DEBATE

turning around
at the front door.

But then—

I see my mother's face
peak through the white lace curtains.

Her eyes go wide.

For a moment I worry
that she won't take me back
after all I put her through.

But the door opens.

# MY FATHER HUGS ME

For the first time
in a long time.

I smell cigarette ash and gin.
So he has picked up new habits.

*Thank God you're back,*
he says.

> I tell him,
> *Your god had nothing to do with*
> *me coming back.*

# MY GOD

is found in air, earth, fire.
In the ocean.

It doesn't matter to me anymore
if my father's god is real.
If he's watching over me
or cursing my every step.

Because no matter what,
I will have to find the courage to be
myself,
completely myself,
for the rest of my life.

Even if that means I am alone.

I know nothing more terrifying
and nothing more freeing.

Not even the ocean.

# I WATCH
# MY FATHER

as he sits back down in his recliner
and rocks back and forth.

I see him for the first time
for what he truly is:

an old man devoid of air, earth, fire, water.
All the things that make us human.

The pity I feel for him
tells me I love him.

I lean down and kiss
his cheek,

and he breaks open.

Tears spill from both of us.

His *sorrys* fill my ears
like water flowing
from an open dam.

That's all I needed
to hear.

# MY MOTHER IS COLD

even though it's warm in the house.

I cannot blame her.
I would freeze too
if the man I loved
broke me.

She leans over the granite countertop,
but doesn't say a thing.

She used to smell warm—
like vanilla and spice.
Now she smells like old roses.

I can almost see invisible thorns
prickling underneath her skin.

*Your father and I are getting a divorce,*
*Dandelion.*
She takes a drag from a Virginia Slim.
Looks like she has new habits, too.

I know better than anyone how pain
can make you do stupid things.

The news lightly grazes my shoulder.
I accept it with peace in my heart.

I cannot change them,
and they cannot change me.

# NEWS OF MY PARENT'S DIVORCE

would have crushed me
a few months ago.

But my cells have renewed themselves
in the course of a summer.

My skin is new.
My heart is open.

And none of the old
gunk that hurt me before
can ever break me again.

# I DO FEEL BAD
# FOR MY MOTHER

Before I left,
she always stood tall
with a ruler-straight spine.

Sure of who she was.

Now here she is,
hunched over.
Smoking a cigarette
and holding back tears.

I am not the only one whose cells have
been replaced this summer.

I just hope for her sake
she can make the most
of this change.

# FOR THE FIRST TIME EVER

I know what it is like to be alone.
It's different than loneliness.

To be lonely is to yearn, it is to ache.
Like an exposed nerve.
Sensitive to the
slightest gust of wind.

To be alone is a choice.
It's looking at the options around you
and deciding your own path
whether or not someone will walk it
with you.

I've been home for a week.
No contact from Andrea or Xavier.

I spend most of my time taking
inspiration from fashion
magazines for my newest outfits.

I'm choosing to be alone,
but I'm not lonely.

# I SEE A PINK
# BABY-DOLL DRESS

in a '90s magazine I picked
up at Silver's.

It reminds me of Andrea.

I nearly text her, but I decide not to.

She will reach out to me
when she is ready.

Until then I will let her
have her space.

# MY SPACE

Here in my room in the last
weeks of summer vacation,

no one else can enjoy the smell
of my new strawberry shampoo.

But I like it.

I am my own company,
and I discover new things about myself.

Little details in my face
or my voice,
things I would have never noticed
if someone else were watching.

Sometimes I talk to myself.
I'm finding my voice and my words.

And sometimes
I turn off all the lights
and start to dance.

# I DANCE LIKE
# A MADMAN

and I dress like one, too.

A '60s mod dress one day.
A '70s leisure suit the next.

Being alone has melted away
any fear of judgment from others.

It's helped me accept and let go
of the anger I've held inside.

What I've been left with
is a real, beating, human heart.

I feel it swell with blessings
that maybe I can share
with the world someday.

# WITH ALL THE LIGHTS OFF

I dance to my favorite song.

The swelling drums and synth beats
send my shoulders up and down.
I twirl and thrash around the room.

The buzz of my phone pauses the song.

Andrea is calling.

# BACK AT ANDREA'S APARTMENT

For a while, we say nothing.

*I like your outfit,*
Andrea offers,
but she is still tense.
Xavier stands behind her.

I'm wearing a studded leather jacket
over a baby-pink tank top
with tight denim jeans.

*Thank you,* I say.
*Listen, I wasn't in my right mind
that day—*

> *I know,*
> she says.
> *But I thought you were over
> what happened
> with Xavier.
> It was one measly night
> three years ago.*

I want to sink to the floor
in shame.
But I'm sick of the version of me
who demanded pity.

And I think of the only thing
I wanted to hear from my dad
when he blew up my whole world.

With all my heart,
I say,
*I really am sorry.*

They look at me, stunned.

*Do you think we can move past this?*

More silence.

   *Give us some time, Eric.*

And I will.
Friends like this are worth
the wait.

# BACK-TO-SCHOOL SEASON

I look through the racks at Silver's
trying to pick out the perfect
first-day outfit.

It'll set the tone for the year.

My mother printed out my
junior year photos
a few days ago for her scrapbook.

In the images, I'm just a shell of a person.
I'm hunched over with an oversized
jacket
and a pained smile.

That wasn't me.
I want people to see who I am
for real.

# PEACE OFFERING

I stare at Andrea's text.

*Xavier and I have tickets to a*
*concert the day before school.*
*Would you like to join us?*

I don't know if our friendship
can be fully fixed.

But I know I will be okay
no matter what happens.

And this is a good step forward.

I text back a smiley face,
and continue with my shopping.

# MY BAG CATCHES

on the door handle
as I'm leaving Silver's.

And I look up to see
the one person I hoped I'd never
have to face again.

Thomas Gregory is on the other side
of the door, watching me struggle.

I look down at my outfit.

He is disgusted.

But I wonder if he feels
much worse about himself
behind closed doors.

# FOR A MOMENT

I feel the eyes of everyone who
has ever judged me
piercing into my skin.

I turn hot.
I worry what
will happen.

Looking at Thomas, I worry
that nothing has changed.

# THEN I REMEMBER

I remember where I've been
and what I've discovered
since we last met—

       my ocean baptism

       Zachary's affection

       the love of my parents

       the forgiveness of my friends

       sweet, fresh coconut water.

Unsticking my bag from the door,
I walk past Thomas,
and out of the store,

alone and with
my head held high.

# WANT TO KEEP READING?

If you liked this book, check out another
book from West 44 Books:

## *RISING OUT*
### BY M. AZMITIA

ISBN: 9781978595439

PART ONE

# The Plan

The first time I
saw Eri,

tumbling
onto the grass at
the park near our
homes,

she was a boy
named Maurice.

She screamed as
she fell.

The Band-Aid
across her nose was
too light.

Tan on deep, dark
brown skin.

I watched her
blood seep through
the Band-Aid.

Watched it
smear with dirt as
she fell again. But

she screamed

and laughed

and stood up again.

I loved her
before I ever knew
what that meant.

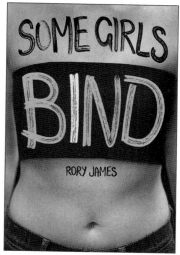

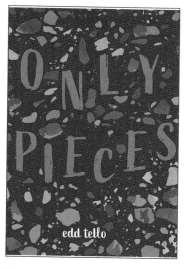

## CHECK OUT MORE BOOKS AT:
www.west44books.com

An imprint of Enslow Publishing

WEST **44** BOOKS™

## About the Author

Angel Barber was born and raised in Buffalo, New York. He is a 19-year-old student at Buffalo State College studying television film arts, with interests in film, philosophy, and psychology. He has written various forms of poetry with the Just Buffalo Writing Center and plans to continue writing and strengthening his poetry and prose well into the future. This is his first novel.